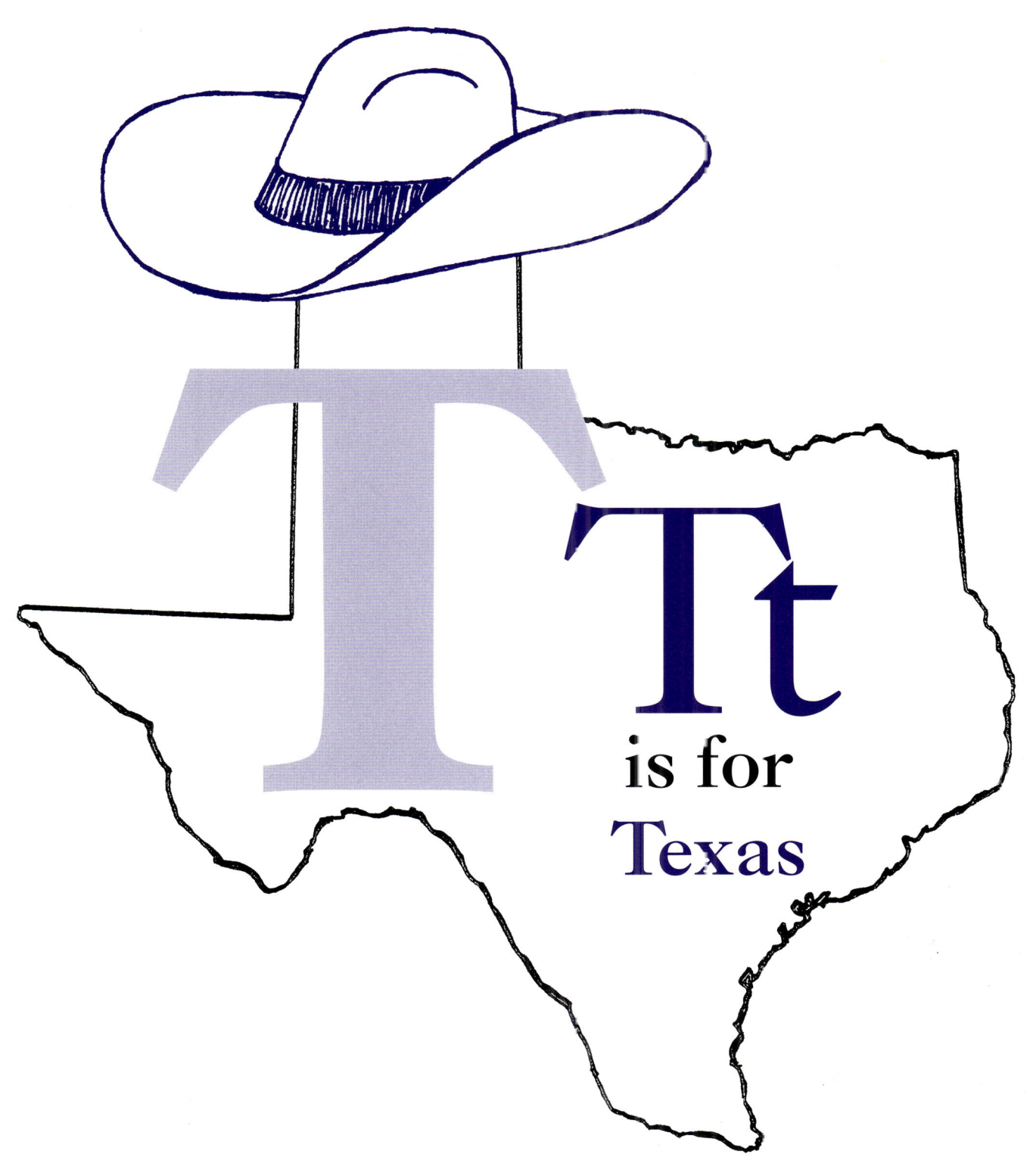

Tt
is for
Texas

Written by Mary D. Wade

Illustrated by Virginia Roeder

Published by GHB Publishers

GHB Publishers, L.L.C.
3906 Old Highway 94 South, Suite 300
St. Charles, MO 63304

Book cover design by Werremeyer |Floresca
Cover illustrations by Virginia Roeder

Manufactured in the United States of America
First Edition

10 9 8 7 6 5 4 3 2 1

Library of Congress Cataloging-in-Publication Data

Wade, Mary D.
T is for Texas / Mary D. Wade ; illustrated by Virginia Roeder.
Saint Charles, Mo : GHB Publishers, c2000.
p. : ill., maps,
Includes index.

Summary: Gives an overview of the state of Texas, including its history,
notable sights, people, and recreations.

Texas--History--Juvenile literature.

Texas.

I. Title   976.4

ISBN 1-892920-28-X

"A" is for the Alamo • "B" is for Big Bend National Park • "C" is for Cattle Drive • "D" is for Dinosaur Valley State Park • "E" is for Enchanted Rock • "F" is for Football • "G" is for Gusher • "H" is for Houston • "I" is for Port Isabel Lighthouse • "J" is for the Johnson Space Center • "K" is for Kian • "L" is for the Lone Star Flag • "M" is for the McDonald Observatory • "N" is for New Braunfels • "O" is for Old Rip • "P" is for Paint Rock • "Q" is for Quanah Parker • "R" is [...] " is for Big Tex • "U" is for Uva[...]ing Crane • "X" is for the X.I.T. [...]abe) Didrikson Zaharias • "A" [...]ark • "C" is for Cattle Drive • [...]or Enchanted Rock • "F" is f[...]ton • "I" is for Port Isabel Lig[...]"K" is for Kian • "L" is for the Lone Star Flag • "M" is for the McDonald Observatory • "N" is for New Braunfels • "O" is for Old Rip • "P" is for Paint Rock • "Q" is for Quanah Parker • "R" is for Rodeo • "S" is for San Felipe de Austin • "T" is for Big Tex • "U" is for Uvalde • "V" is for the Vereins Kirche • "W" is for Whooping Crane • "X" is for the X.I.T. Ranch • "Y" is for Ysleta • "Z" is for Mildred (Babe) Didrikson Zaharias • "A" is for the Alamo • "B" is for Big Bend

For Harold,
who brought me Texas
— M.D.W.

For Pratt, Andrew, and Emily,
who already know their ABCs
but may discover wonderful
new things about Texas
— V.R.

TEXAS STATE SYMBOLS

Bird	Mockingbird
Dish	Chili
Fabric and Fiber	Cotton
Fish	Guadalupe Bass
Flower	Bluebonnet
Gem	Texas Blue Topaz
Insect	Monarch Butterfly
Large Mammal	Longhorn
Small Mammal	Armadillo
Pepper	Jalapeño
Plant	Prickly Pear Cactus
Tree	Pecan

Motto	"Friendship"
Nickname	"Lone Star State"
Song	"Texas, Our Texas"
State Capital	Austin

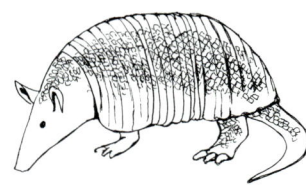

TEXAS *history*

Texas is a big state. It is 801 miles from north to south, and 733 miles from east to west. It has mountains, plains, deserts, forests, and saltwater beaches. Until Alaska joined the United States, Texas was the largest state. Among its cities are three of the top ten population centers in the nation.

The earliest inhabitants lived in Texas about 30,000 years ago, but the first recorded contact was made in the 1500s by a shipwrecked Spanish conquistador named Cabeza de Vaca. The Caddo group, who then resided in Texas, called themselves "Tayshas," meaning "allies" or "friends." The Spaniards spelled the group's name T-E-J-A-S. That is how Texas got its name and its motto, "friendship."

The largest part of the Texas population today is of European ancestry, including a large number of German descent. Many with African heritage are descendants of former slaves. More recently many Asians have come to Texas. Not surprisingly a large part of the population is Hispanic.

Texas was once part of Mexico. In the 1820s, Stephen Austin brought the first Anglo settlers to Texas. Fifteen years later the Texans broke with Mexico and formed a republic that lasted ten years. Finally in 1845, Texans voted to join the Union.

Although many Texans did not wish to leave the Union, Texas sided with the Confederacy during the Civil War. The last battle of the war was fought at the southern tip of Texas, one month after Confederate forces had surrendered.

Texas is known for cowboys. The famous cattle drives began with wild longhorn herds being driven north from Texas. The state normally leads all others in numbers of cattle and sheep. It leads in the production of wool (from sheep) and mohair (from goats). It also usually leads in the production of cotton. In addition, Texas is a major producer of citrus crops and pecans.

The oil industry has brought much money to Texas. Unlike other states, Texas gets to keep money from its offshore wells because of an agreement it made when it joined the Union.

Under that same agreement, Texas could divide itself into five states if the people chose to do so. That's not likely to happen. Texans are proud of their state. There are even bumper stickers that say, "I wasn't born in Texas, but I got here as fast as I could."

3

AAa is for the Alamo.

San Antonio •

The most famous place in Texas is the Alamo.

The battle at the Alamo helped make Texas a free country. The part of the Alamo everyone recognizes is actually the chapel of the old mission. Today the Alamo is in downtown San Antonio, and the chapel is a museum.

BBb

is for
**Big Bend
National Park.**

Big Bend
National Park

The Rio Grande River takes a big bend as it forms the border between the United States and Mexico. Big Bend National Park sits in the tip. The river has

cut deep canyons with walls that plunge straight down over 1,800 feet. Among the fossils found in the park is the largest known pterosaur.

Cc is for cattle drive.

Canyon

Cowboys drove Texas cattle to the railroads in Kansas.

8

A steer named Old Blue led the drives for the Charles Goodnight herd. When they got to the railroad, he stepped aside. The other cattle went to the meatpackers, but Old Blue returned to the ranch. His long horns are in the Panhandle-Plains Museum in Canyon.

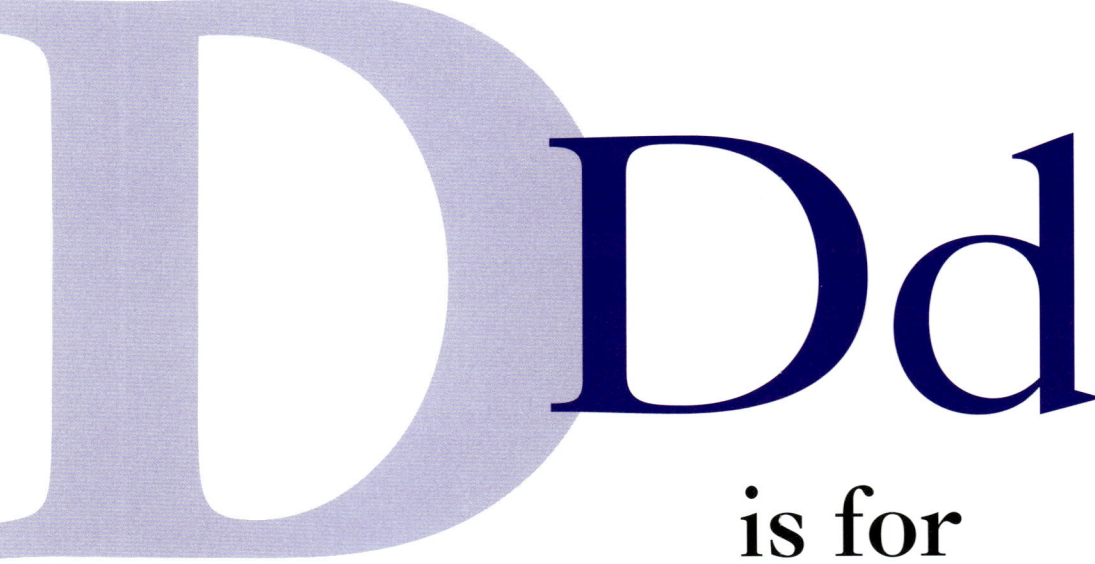

DDd is for Dinosaur Valley State Park.

Dinosaur Valley
State Park

About 100 million years ago, dinosaurs walked in soft mud.

Their tracks turned to stone, which today can be seen in the bed of the Paluxy River near Glen Rose. The tracks range from 12 to 36 inches long and 9 to 24 inches wide. They were made by dinosaurs called acrocanthosaurus, pleurocoelus, and iguanodon.

Ee

Enchanted Rock

is for Enchanted Rock.

12

In central Texas, a smooth mass of pink granite rises about 385 feet above the ground. It is called Enchanted Rock, and it is the second largest such rock formation in the United States. The Comanche and Tonkawa Indians thought it was sacred. Some people thought it was haunted. Enchanted Rock makes groaning sounds when the rock cools after the sun goes down.

13

Ff is for football.

People in Texas love football. Even high school games bring out crowds of people.

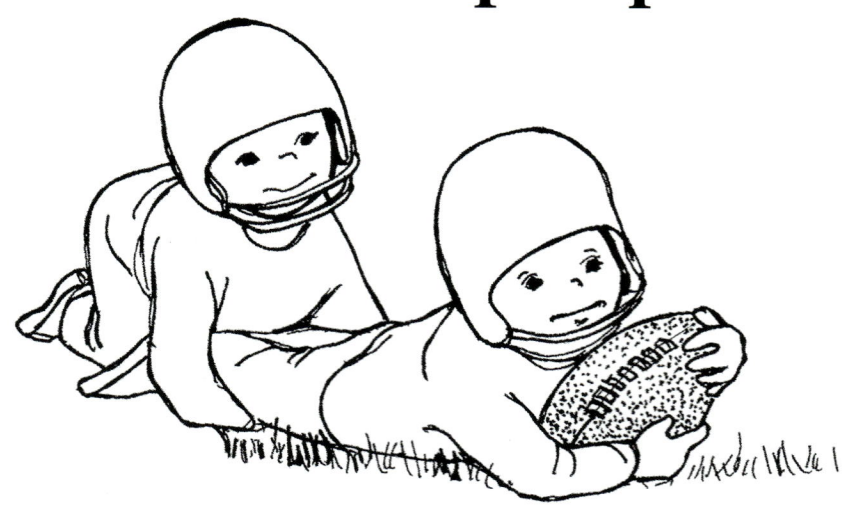

Cheerleaders and bands keep the spirit going. In small towns where there aren't enough players for a regular team, the game is played with only six players. The Dallas Cowboys professional team is often called "America's Team."

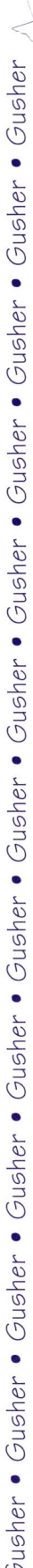

G g

is for gusher.

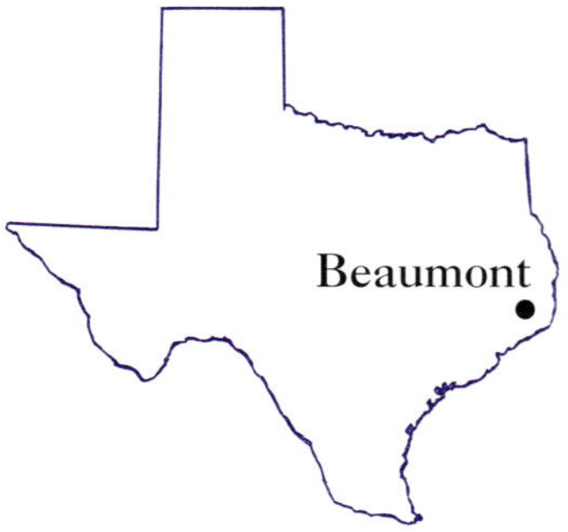

Beaumont

Early oil wells were sometimes gushers. A black spray of oil blew over the top of the derrick when the drillers broke through the rocks to the pool of oil. Near Beaumont, a gusher at Spindletop "blew in" on January 10, 1901. This started the race to find oil in Texas. Big fields developed in the Panhandle, West Texas, and even in the Gulf of Mexico.

H Hh
is for
Sam Houston.

Huntsville
Houston

Sam Houston directed the battle that won Texas independence from Mexico.

18

He was the first president of the Republic of Texas. Later he was a U.S. senator and then the governor of Texas. The city of Houston is named for him. There is a huge statue of Sam Houston on Interstate 45 near Huntsville, one of the towns where he lived.

HOUSTON

Port Isabel Lighthouse • Port Isabel Lighthouse • Port Isabel Lighthouse • Port Isabel Lighthouse • Port Isabel Lighthouse • Port Isabel Lighthouse

Ii is for Port Isabel Lighthouse.

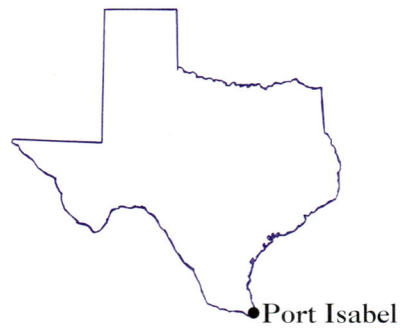

Port Isabel

PORT ISABEL LIGHTHOUSE

STATE HISTORIC STRUCTURE
TEXAS PARKS & WILDLIFE DEPARTMENT

The Port Isabel Lighthouse was built in 1853 across from the tip of South Padre Island.

During the Civil War, the lamp was buried and never found. The lighthouse had many repairs and was completely restored when it was 100 years old. Its mercury-vapor light helps ships navigate. Today visitors can climb to the top of the lighthouse.

J Jj

is for the **Johnson Space Center.**

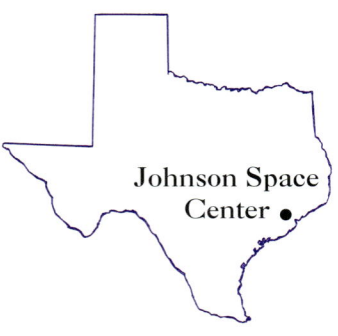

Johnson Space
Center

Johnson
Space Center
is about
20 miles
south of
Houston.

It is named for President Lyndon B. Johnson, a native Texan. Mission Control at the Space Center guides NASA's flights. At the visitor center, people can watch engineers track flights. Visitors can also walk around rockets, see equipment, and learn how astronauts train.

23

Kk is for Kian.

Bolivar Peninsula

Jane Long, who is called the "Mother of Texas," had a slave named Kian.

After everyone else had left Bolivar Peninsula, they survived without help during the bitter winter of 1821.

Later Kian helped Jane run boarding houses. Kian chose to stay with Jane after slavery ended. When Jane was a very old woman, she would not let anyone but Kian's grand-daughter, who was also named Kian, take care of her.

L1 is for the **Lone Star flag.**

Austin

The land that makes up Texas has had six different flags flying over it, but the Lone Star flag has been used since the time Texas was a country.

It was adopted in 1839 in Austin, the state capital. The flag has only one star, so people call Texas the "Lone Star State." Texas is the only state in the nation that can fly its flag at the same height as the United States flag.

MMm

is for the **McDonald Observatory.**

McDonald
Observatory

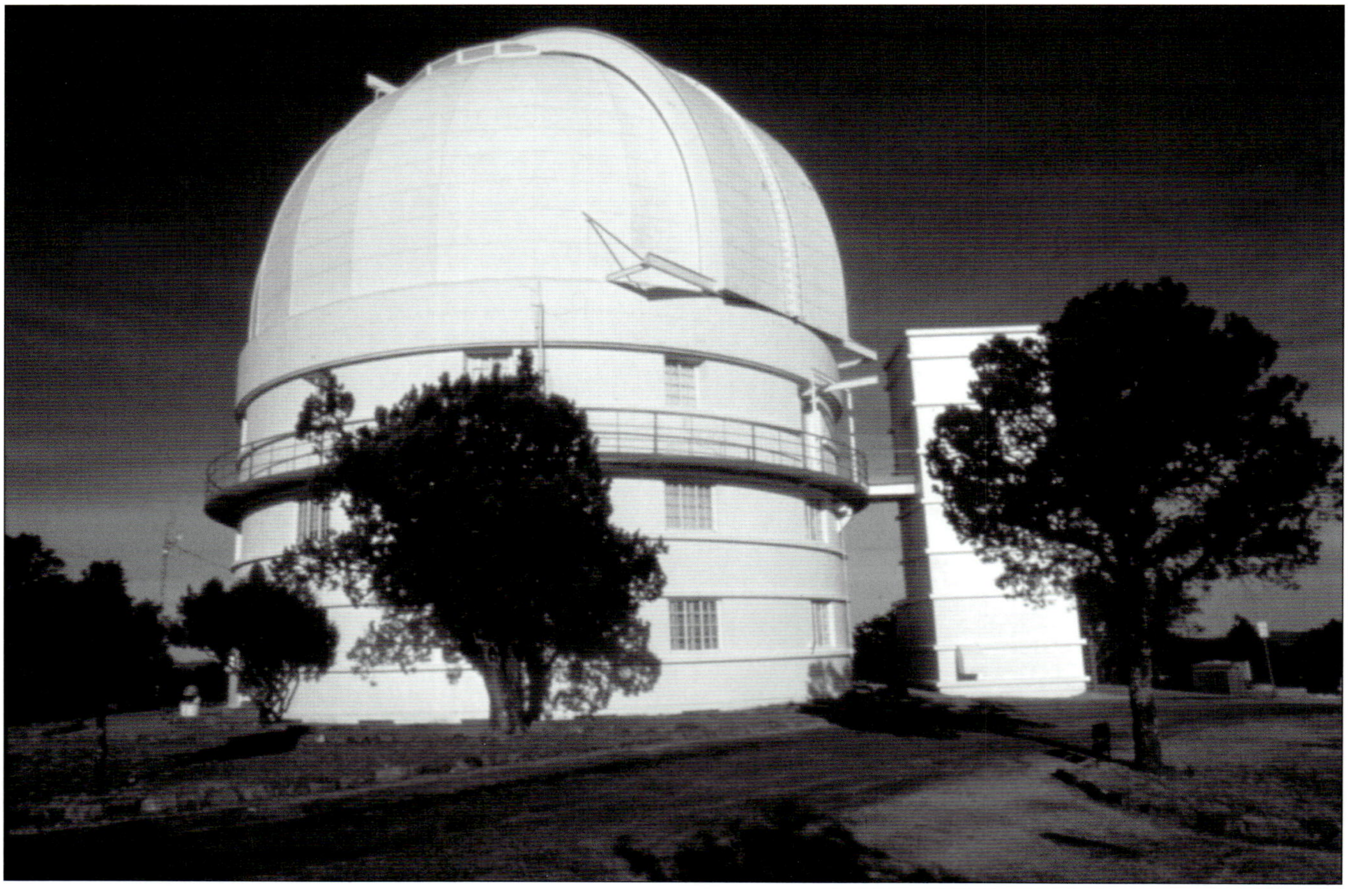

The McDonald Observatory sits 6,781 feet above sea level, away from city lights and polluted air. The stars and planets are easy to see in West Texas. The observatory is named for the man who gave money to the University of Texas to build it. McDonald Observatory's first telescope was the second largest telescope in the world at that time. Now the observatory has a reflector telescope with a 107-inch lens.

N

Nn
is for
New Braunfels.

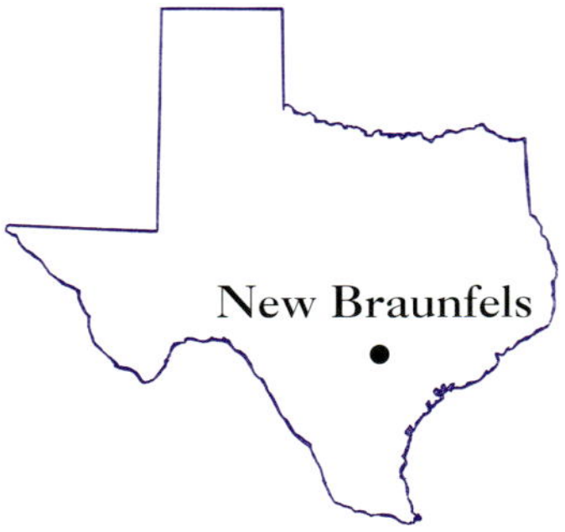

New Braunfels

New Braunfels was settled by German immigrants in the 1840s.

Good water attracted new people to the city then, and it still does. The state's shortest river, the Comal, bubbles out of the ground in the city park. It flows into the Guadalupe River two and a half miles away. Fun seekers enjoy floating down the Guadalupe on rubber tubes.

Oo

is for **Old Rip**.

Eastland

The Eastland County courthouse was built 100 years ago.

Officials sealed things inside a cornerstone to mark the event. Thirty years later they opened the cornerstone and found a live horned toad! The toad was named "Old Rip" after Rip Van Winkle. Old Rip made national news. He is now in a glass-front casket in the new courthouse.

P

is for
Paint Rock.

Pp

• Paint Rock

People began gathering at a special place beside the Concho River beginning in ancient times.

34

While they were there, they made red and black drawings. It is easy to recognize those drawings representing people, circles, stars, and buffalo, but some of the shapes cannot be explained. A shape that looks like a Spanish mission probably represented the San Sabá Mission that was destroyed in the 1750s. It was located not far from Paint Rock.

Qq

is for
Quanah Parker.

Quanah

Quanah, the son of a Comanche chief and Cynthia Ann Parker, escaped capture when soldiers returned his mother to her relatives 26 years after she had been taken from them.

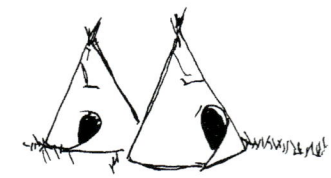

36

He never saw her again. Quanah became a Comanche chief. After the buffalo were gone, he was forced to take his people to the reservation. This strong leader showed them how to live in the white man's world. Quanah had many friends, including President Teddy Roosevelt. The town of Quanah is named for him.

R

Rr is for rodeo.

Stamford

Rodeos were originally held to show off skills cowboys used on the ranch.

Today rodeo events include roping, bronc and bull riding, barrel-racing, and even concerts from country and western singers. Often there is a competition among prize livestock. Young people participate in the calf scramble in hopes of winning a calf. There are rodeos held all over Texas. The world's largest amateur rodeo, the Texas Cowboy Reunion, is held every 4th of July weekend in Stamford.

Ss is for San Felipe de Austin.

San Felipe

Stephen F. Austin, the "Father of Texas," brought the first Anglo settlers to Texas in the 1820s.

At his headquarters in San Felipe, Austin assigned the settlers their land. The little town was destroyed during the Texas Revolution, but the state park on the banks of the Brazos River has a replica of Austin's log cabin.

Tt is for Big Tex.

Dallas

Big Tex welcomes visitors to the Texas State Fair in Dallas each fall.

Every year the huge figure gets a new set of cowboy clothes. Big Tex stands in "Big Tex Circle" near the midway of the fair. The fairgrounds were built to celebrate the Texas centennial in 1936. Some buildings on the grounds are open year-round. They house an aquarium and museums of science and history.

U

Uu
is for **Uvalde.**

Uvalde

Uvalde, birthplace of Vice-President John Nance Garner, is a beautiful area of southwest Texas with hills and flowing rivers.

The town was named for Spaniard Juan de Ugalde, who was appointed governor of the area in 1776. In Spanish, the letter "g" is pronounced like the letter "h." Later American settlers changed the "g" in Ugalde to a "v," which was easier for them to pronounce.

45

V

Vv is for the Vereins Kirche (Society Church).

Fredericksburg

A society sent settlers from Germany to Texas in the 1840s. The settlers made a treaty with the Comanches and started the town of Fredericksburg.

They built the Vereins Kirche to use for church services and a school. Today a replica of this eight-sided building stands on Main Street. In 1996, Comanches came from Oklahoma to Fredericksburg to help celebrate the town's 150th anniversary.

Ww

is for
whooping crane.

Aransas Pass

Whooping cranes are the largest birds in North America.

They are solid white except for black wing tips that show when they fly. Whooping cranes are endangered. Every year they fly from Canada to spend the winter at Aransas Pass Wildlife Refuge. Each family of whoopers claims a square mile area of coastal marsh as its own.

Xx is for the X.I.T. Ranch.

Dalhart •

When Texans needed money for a new capitol building in 1888, they traded three million acres of land in the Panhandle to pay for it.

The X.I.T. Ranch was formed on this land. It was so large that a cowboy could ride for two weeks without seeing anyone else. Years later the land was sold to make smaller ranches. In Dalhart, a rodeo and a museum preserve the spirit and history of the X.I.T. Ranch.

Y Yy

is
for
Ysleta.

El Paso

Ysleta is the oldest town in Texas. It was in Mexico until the Rio Grande River changed its course. Now it is surrounded by El Paso. The Tigua (Tee-wah) Indians settled Ysleta more than 300 years ago. They still make bread using a centuries-old recipe and bake it in beehive ovens.

Zz is for Mildred (Babe) Didrikson Zaharias.

Port Arthur

Mildred "Babe" Zaharias was born in Port Arthur in 1914.

She got her nickname from school boys who thought she batted like Babe Ruth. She excelled in basketball, track and field, and golf. At the 1932 Olympics, Babe broke world records in the javelin throw, hurdles, and high jump. Some consider her the greatest woman athlete who ever lived.

INDEX

SUGGESTED READINGS

Kim Simon, former owner of the children's book wholesaler Reading Express, suggests the following titles to further expand a child's library on Texas:

Babe Didrikson Zaharias: All-Around Athlete
Written by Jane Sutcliffe
Illustrated by Jeni Reeves
Published by Lerner Books
Focuses on important episodes in Zaharias' life that show what kind of person she was.

Bill Pickett: Rodeo-Ridin' Cowboy
Written by Andrea D. Pinkney
Illustrated by Brian Pinkney
Published by Harcourt Brace
A story of the famous African American cowboy who grew up in Texas watching the cowboys drive cattle along the Chisholm Trail.

Susanna of the Alamo: A True Story
Written by John Jakes
Illustrated by Paul Bacon
Published by Harcourt Brace
Relates the experiences of the Texas woman, who, along with her baby, survived the 1836 massacre at the Alamo.

White Dynamite and Curly Kidd
Written by Bill Martin Jr and John Archambault
Illustrated by Ted Rand
Published by Henry Holt
"A rollicking ride for rodeo bronc buster Curly Kidd — and for young listeners. The rhythmic language and the energetic illustrations make for a dynamite presentation." — *School Library Journal*, starred review

PHOTO ACKNOWLEDGMENTS

Grateful acknowledgment is expressed to the following for permission to reprint their photographs in "T" is for Texas:

A — Jack Lewis/TxDOT.

B — Jack Lewis/TxDOT.

C — Jack Lewis/TxDOT.

D — Bob Parvin/TxDOT.

E — Jack Lewis/TxDOT.

F — Al Bello/Allsport.

G — Courtesy of Texas Energy Museum, Inc.

H — Courtesy of TxDOT.

I — Richard Reynolds/TxDOT.

J — Gay Shackelford/TxDOT.

K — Courtesy of The UT-Institute of Texan Cultures at San Antonio.

L — AP/Wide World Photos.

M — Kevin Stillman/TxDOT.

N — J. Griffis Smith/TxDOT.

O — Courtesy of H.V. O'Brien.

P — Jack Lewis/TxDOT.

Q — Courtesy of the Panhandle-Plains Historical Museum.

R — Jack Lewis/TxDOT.

S — Jack Lewis/TxDOT.

T — Jack Lewis/TxDOT.

U — Jack Lewis/TxDOT.

V — Courtesy of Gillespie County Historical Museum, Fredericksburg.

W — Bill Reaves/TxDOT.

X — Bob Parvin/TxDOT.

Y — Courtesy of TxDOT.

Z — Courtesy of Babe Didrikson Zaharias Foundation, Inc.